Ed's Egg

by David Bedford
Illustrated by Karen Sapp

Sandy Creek
NEW YORK

Ed loved being an egg.

Ed jumped up and down...

Ed rolled around and around,
and stood on his shiny
egg head.

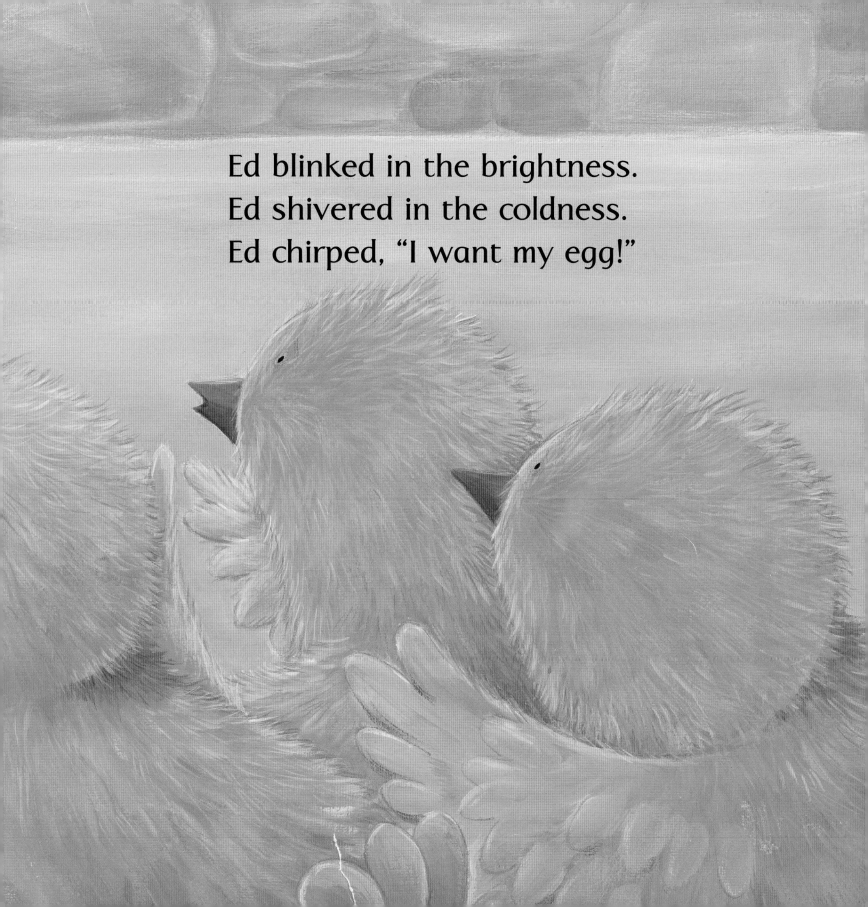

Ed blinked in the brightness.
Ed shivered in the coldness.
Ed chirped, "I want my egg!"

Ed did his best to put his
egg back together.

It wasn't too bad, thought Ed.
He could see out, and no one
could see in.

Then Ed heard
a noise...

It was two big ducks, SPLISH-SPLASHING.

Ed could see them, but they couldn't see Ed, because Ed was still in his egg.

So Ed joined in the splish-splashing, until...

Three frogs came HOPPITY-HOPPING!

Ed could see them, but they couldn't see Ed,
because Ed was still in his egg.

So Ed joined in the hoppity-hopping, until...

Four mice were TUMBLY-BOUNCING.

Ed could see them, but they couldn't see
Ed, because Ed was still in his egg.

Ed joined in the tumbly-bouncing all by himself.

And he didn't notice something BIG cluck-cluck-clucking...

Ed tried to hide in his egg, but...
where was it?

Ed shivered. There was
nowhere to hide.

The BIG cluck-cluck-clucker
looked down, and little Ed looked up.
He saw happy eyes and a smiley
beak, and he knew it must be...

"Mom!"

"Hooray!" chirped Ed's brothers
and sisters. "Ed is out of his egg."

Ed played SPLISH-SPLASHING, HOPPITY-HOPPING, and TUMBLY-BOUNCING!

It was fun being out of his egg.

But when he was tired...

Ed wished he still had somewhere cozy
and safe to go.

"We know!" said his brothers
and sisters. "Follow us."
And Ed soon found out that...

"Moms are better than eggs,"
he chirped.

Sandy Creek
NEW YORK

An Imprint of Sterling Publishing
387 Park Avenue South
New York, NY 10016

Text © 2010 by QEB Publishing, Inc.
Illustrations © 2010 by QEB Publishing, Inc.

This 2012 edition published by Sandy Creek

Editor: Amanda Askew
Designers: Vida and Luke Kelly

ISBN 978-1-4351-3081-4

Manufactured in China
Lot #:
10 9 8 7 6 5 4 3
11/12